This book belongs to

_____

_____

For Daniel
J.E.

To Ollie and Paddy
T.T.

First published in 2006 in Great Britain by Gullane Children's Books
This paperback edition published in 2006 by
Gullane Children's Books
an imprint of Pinwheel Limited
Winchester House, 259-269 Old Marylebone Road,
London NW1 5XJ

1 3 5 7 9 10 8 6 4 2

Text © Jonathan Emmett 2006
Illustrations © Thomas Taylor 2006

The right of Jonathan Emmett and Thomas Taylor to be identified as the author and illustrator of this work
has been asserted by them in accordance with the Copyright, Designs, and Patents Act, 1988.
A CIP record for this title is available from the British Library.

ISBN-13: 978-1-86233-590-5
ISBN-10: 1-86233-590-7

Printed and bound in Singapore

Rabbit's Day Off!

Jonathan Emmett

illustrated by Thomas Taylor

GULLANE
CHILDREN'S BOOKS

Brrringgg - brrringgg!

Brrringgg - brrringgg!

It was early in the morning.
The telephone was ringing.
And it was Rabbit's day off.

"Rabbit!" called a voice down the telephone. "It's Badger! Would you mind running the train down to Sycamore Station? It's for something important!"

"I wouldn't mind," yawned Rabbit, "but —"
"Splendid!" said Badger, and he put down the phone.

Rabbit hurried about the engine, tweaking and twiddling things, until everything was ready to go. He stoked the fire, topped up the boiler, oiled all the pistons, and greased all the wheels.

Clickety-clack! Clickety-clack!

The train set off along the track.

It was a beautiful day for a train ride
– but it was Rabbit's day off!
"I wouldn't mind," he told himself, "but today — "

Sccrrreeeecccchh!

The train came squealing to a stop.

"Oh my brush and bristles!" said Squirrel. "Are you all right?"
"I am," said Rabbit. "But I must get the train to Sycamore Station. It's for something important!"
"Ah!" said Squirrel. "I'll see what I can do."

Squirrel scampered about the bridge, fiddling and fixing things,

until everything was mended.

Rabbit was so pleased – he gave Squirrel a ride.

Clickety-clack! Clickety-clack!

The train set off along the track.

It was a beautiful day for a train ride - the fire was blazing
- but it was Rabbit's day off!
"I wouldn't mind," he told Squirrel, "but today happens — "

Scccrrreeeecccchh!
The train came squealing to a stop.

"Oh my teeth and toenails!" said Beaver.
"Are you all right?"
"We are," said Rabbit. "But I must get
the train to Sycamore Station!"
"It's for something important!" added
Squirrel, winking at Beaver.
"Ah!" said Beaver. "I'll see what I can do."

Beaver bustled about the fallen tree, nibbling and gnawing things,

until everything was cleared away.

Rabbit was so pleased – he gave Beaver a ride.

Clickety-clack! Clickety-clack!

The train set off along the track.

It was a beautiful day for a train ride – the fire was blazing,
the boiler was bubbling – but it was Rabbit's day off!
"I wouldn't mind," he told Beaver, "but today happens to – "

Sccrrreeeeecccchh!
The train came squealing to a stop.

"Oh my fur and fingers!" said Mole.
"Are you all right?"
"We are," said Rabbit. "But I must
get the train to the station!"
"It's for something important!" added
Squirrel and Beaver, winking at Mole.
"Ah!" said Mole. "I'll see what I can do."

Mole moved about the tunnel, scraping and scooping things,

until everything was cleared out.

Rabbit was so pleased – he gave Mole a ride too.

Clickety-clack! Clickety-clack!
The train set off along the track.

It was a beautiful day for a train ride – the fire was blazing, the boiler was bubbling, the pistons were pumping – but it was Rabbit's day off!

"I wouldn't mind," he told Mole, "but today happens to be — "

"YOUR BIRTHDAY!" shouted all the others, as the train slowed to a stop.

"Happy Birthday Rabbit!" said Badger.
"Oh my *goodness!*" said Rabbit, who didn't know
what to do with himself.
"I told you it was something important!" smiled
Badger. "Now sit back and enjoy the ride!"

Clickety-clack! Clickety-clack!
The train set off along the track.

It was a beautiful day for a train ride - the fire was blazing, the boiler was bubbling, the pistons were pumping and the wheels were whirring along the track

- AND it was Rabbit's **BIRTHDAY!**

"It looked like the train might never get to the station," laughed Squirrel

"It was one problem after another," agreed Beaver.

"But we sorted them all out," said Mole.

"I hope you didn't mind, Rabbit," whispered Badger.

"After all, it was your day off."

Rabbit said nothing.
He just twitched his nose happily
and ate another piece of cake.

Other Gullane Children's Books
for you to enjoy . . .

Pugwug and Little

Susie Jenkin-Pearce • Tina Macnaughton

Happy Birthday Santa!

Gillian Rogerson • Ingela Peterson

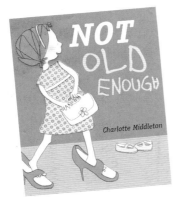

Not old Enough

Charlotte Middleton

An Itch To Scratch

Damian Harvey • Lynne Chapman